ANIMORPHS®

ALTERNAMORPHS

The First Journey

Look for other **ANIMORPHS**®
titles by K.A. Applegate:

ALTERNAMORPHS

The First Journey

K.A. Applegate

AN
APPLE
PAPERBACK

SCHOLASTIC INC.
New York Toronto London Auckland Sydney
Mexico City New Delhi Hong Kong

No part of this publication may be reproduced in whole or in part, or stored in a retrieval system, or transmitted in any form or by any means, electronic, mechanical, photocopying, recording, or otherwise, without written permission of the publisher. For information regarding permission, write to Scholastic Inc., Attention: Permissions Department, 555 Broadway, New York, NY 10012.

ISBN 0-439-06164-4

Copyright © 1999 by Scholastic Inc., based on the ANIMORPHS® book series by K.A. Applegate. All rights reserved. Published by Scholastic Inc. APPLE PAPERBACKS, SCHOLASTIC, ANIMORPHS and associated logos are trademarks and/or registered trademarks of Scholastic Inc.

12 11 10 9 8 7 6 5 4 3 2 1   9/9 0 1 2 3 4/0

Printed in the U.S.A.

First Scholastic printing, April 1999

For Tonya Alicia Martin,
who morphed this idea into reality

ALTERNAMORPHS

The First Journey

Introduction

Okay, listen up. It's Jake. You probably already know what's going on around here. But just in case you don't, here's the deal: Rachel, Tobias, Cassie, Marco, Ax, and I are five kids and one alien out to save the world.

No, this isn't a joke. It's real. About as real as you can get. Real enough for screaming nightmares about the things you've seen and done.

Because sometimes the stuff you see in the movies, the stuff you thought could never, ever happen to you . . . well, it *can* happen. It *does* happen. I've seen it.

I can't tell you my last name. Or where I live. There's an alien invasion going on. Right here on Earth. But I'm not talking little green guys with ray guns. I'm talking a much smarter way to conquer a world. Just invade people's brains.

I'm not nuts. I've seen it. And because of

that, my friends and I were given a special power — the power to morph into *any* animal we touch. To acquire its DNA. It's the only way we can fight the Yeerks — that's what they call themselves. We have to find a way to stop these slugs that get into people's heads and make them slaves.

But things have gotten worse. We need backup. A new Animorph. We've tried this once before and it didn't work out. At all. We're going to try again. So, if you're interested in joining us, let's go. Just remember not to read these missions like a normal book. Check out the instructions and follow them.

You get to choose your morphs, but I'm warning you now — choose them *very* carefully. You have to deal with the consequences. They can either help you, or get you totally annihilated.

This isn't a game. It's serious stuff. So if you can handle it, turn to page one.

Oh. One more thing? Good luck.

You'll need it.

CHAPTER 1

You know you shouldn't be doing it. You were supposed to be home at least twenty minutes ago. It's getting dark. The smart thing to do, the only thing, really, is to ride your bike along the bike path like a law-abiding citizen. All the way home.

But you don't. You're an off-road cycling freak, so you head for the construction site across from the mall. How many times have you been told *not* to do that? Like a million. "It's dangerous," your mom says. Deep pits filled with water, cinder block obstacles, dips, and downhill runs.

In other words, highly cool.

2

Last Saturday you chose a spot and yanked away the worst debris. You made this sort of single-track loop. It has a killer rolling dip and a log made out of cinder blocks that you can jump. When you're on it, you pretend that you're racing in one of the mountain biking clubs your mom won't let you join because they're too dangerous.

Too dangerous? Just wait, Mom. Have I got a story for you. Only I can never, *ever* tell you. Or anyone else.

Anyway, that night, there you are. Going around and around the track, faster and faster. There's just barely enough light to see.

Out of the corner of your eye, you see some dark forms moving. You stop your bike, a little nervous. You think it could be a band of home-less men who live here. But then you recognize kids from school, kids you know. Jake, Marco, Cassie, Rachel, and Tobias. You don't know them that well, except maybe Marco. He sits next to you in science and makes jokes under his breath all during class. Thanks to him, you're barely breaking a C.

You think about yelling "hey!" but you don't want to scare them. And they look like such a group, somehow. You didn't know they were all friends. You feel a little bit left out, even though they didn't see you. You aren't terribly swell at making friends.

Maybe because you spend most of your time riding around and around a makeshift track.

The group moves away, and you keep circling the track, trying to get in some killer laps before dinner.

You're rounding the track for the last time, flying over the cinder block log, when you see it. A light. It's moving fast, way faster than an airplane or helicopter. And you'd have to call the light *blue,* even though you don't think you've ever seen that shade of blue, somehow. It's a blue that is almost white, and yet it registers as more blue than any blue you've ever seen.

That doesn't make much sense, but neither does the light.

You stand there, your mouth open like a fish, and watch it come closer. You see that the light has a shape. It's like an egg with two stubby wings. The blue light is coming from a shaft at the end. And suddenly, you get what it is.

It's a UFO. You know it. And it isn't because you watch the *X-Files.* It's because every hair on your head is standing on end.

Instead of running away, like a normal person, you run *toward* it. You keep out of sight be-

4

hind a tumble of masonry and cinder blocks. That's when you see Jake, Tobias, Marco, Cassie, and Rachel. Rachel's hair is standing straight out from her head, so at least you're not alone.

Your heart pounds as the UFO lands. The kids huddle together. You can't hear them, but you know they're wondering what to do, like you are.

Then you hear Tobias's voice.

"Please, come out. We won't hurt you."

<I know.>

The voice was in your head! You didn't hear it with your ears.

Marco and Jake exchange glances. Tobias looks at Rachel. They all stare at each other, wide-eyed. They've heard it, too!

Tobias asks if the voice will come out, and he replies yes. He warns you not to be frightened.

You peer through a crack in the half-wall. A creature steps out of the ship. For a minute, you think of a ballet dancer. Which is crazy, because this creature has hooves. Four of them. And blue fur, and four eyes, two of them on two little horns that come out of his head. A head with no mouth. No wonder the guy talks to your brain.

Oh, and the tail. You can't keep your eyes off it. Or rather, the long stinger on the end of it that looks as though it could do some serious damage.

Here's the funny thing: You're not that scared. Not really. First of all, there's a nice solid wall between you and the alien. And somehow, you suspect he won't harm you.

<You're right,> you hear in your head. <So you can come out. You don't have to hide.>

You gaze around wildly.

<Yes, I'm talking to you,> he says.

And that part about not being scared? Forget about it. Now, you're terrified.

CHAPTER 2

You step out from behind the wall.

"Whoa," Marco says. "Another alien. Let the games begin."

But his voice shakes a little, and you know he's scared, too.

You stand next to the others. The alien stumbles a bit and then falls, and you realize that he's hurt.

<I am dying,> he says.

Then he tells you about the Yeerks. How they've invaded Earth by taking over humans. How their sluglike bodies invade people's brains.

It all sounds crazy. And terrifying. You're relieved to hear that the Andalites — which is what the creature calls himself — are fighting the Yeerks.

That means somebody else is taking care of it. You don't have to worry.

<Yes, you do.>

He is the last Andalite, he tells you. It may take a year before the rest of them return. By that time, the Yeerks will have taken over the Earth and all its people.

"What?" you blurt out. "That's impossible!"

<I have seen what they are capable of,> the Andalite replies, and you turn stone-cold at the way he says it.

There is one thing he can do to help before he dies. The Andalite directs Jake to fetch a small blue box from his ship. Jake looks a little nervous, but he disappears inside, then reappears holding the box.

The Andalite tells you that he can give you the power to morph into any animal you choose. You just have to touch the animal to require its DNA.

"You've got to be kidding," Marco says.

You can't believe it, either. It's way past wacky. Way past unreal.

Suddenly, you see red lights in the sky. Rachel sees them, too.

<Yeerks,> the Andalite says. The hatred in his

8

voice is like a living force. He calls the ships Bug fighters. <Hurry.>

You place your hand on the box next to the others. Six hands, and then the Andalite's. You feel a shock wave run from your fingers up your arm, into your body. It doesn't hurt. It feels . . . nice. Like a warm buzz of comfort.

But then a third ship appears alongside the red lights. It is larger. Blacker than black, it is like a piece of a starless night sky. It is a strange shape.

Jake says it's like a medieval battle-ax. Rolling out from its surface is a feeling that you can only describe as evil. You've never felt this before. But you know what it is.

<Go now,> the Andalite warns. <They cannot find you. And remember, you can only stay in animal morph for two hours or you will be trapped in your morph forever. Now go! Visser Three is with them in the Blade ship. Run!>

Tobias stays behind for a moment, but the rest of you take off. You feel the urgency and the power of the Andalite's order.

Suddenly, you see your hand glow. You realize that your hand is in the circle of white-hot light coming from the ship. A searchlight!

You snatch your hand back, out of the light,

and run. With a burst of strength, the six of you leap over the half-wall. Your knees hit the ground hard, but you hardly feel the pain.

Now, the searchlight from the ship illuminates the dying Andalite. The Bug fighters slowly descend.

There is nothing you can do. Nothing.

You watch as Visser Three exits the black Blade ship. You see the creatures called Hork-Bajir, walking weapons with blades growing out of their wrists and elbows. They serve as hosts for the Yeerks. And then the enormous, spidery Taxxons, evil creatures who willingly allowed the Yeerks to take over their brains and horrible bodies.

Fear grips you. You've never known fear like this. A Hork-Bajir comes close, so close you could toss a stone and hit it. You hold your breath. You want to scream, you want to run. You have to get away. . . .

But you feel something warm seep in, like a curl of warm water swirling around you. The Andalite has sent you courage.

You need the courage. Because you have to watch him die.

In a sneering voice, Visser Three calls him Prince Elfangor. He morphs into a creature more horrible than the Taxxons, taller, bigger, with teeth three feet long. Their points are sharp as daggers.

The fight is horrible. Already dying, the prince fights bravely. You can see there is no hope for him. And there is no mercy in Visser Three. Cassie covers her eyes. Rachel stares straight ahead, her eyes blazing hatred.

Visser Three opens that deadly mouth with the teeth like steel spikes. Jake almost springs to help, but you help Rachel pull him back. No one can help.

At the last very moment, you turn away. You can't bear to see Prince Elfangor die. Not like that.

But you hear it. You hear the scream in your head. It is more awful than anything you've ever heard. Tobias leans over and gags.

The nearest Hork-Bajir turns at the sound. You see his eyes rake the darkness. You know he is listening.

You don't know who springs up first. But suddenly, you can't contain the terror any longer, and you all take off. Running as fast as you ever knew you could run.

"Split up!" Jake yells, and you veer away from the others.

You know the construction site pretty well. The prince had said that Hork-Bajir don't see very well in the dark, so you hug the shadows. You can hear one of them behind you, his blades whistling through the air. He is very fast.

You stumble over a piece of rusted equipment. The Hork-Bajir is close, closer. He can't see you, but he can hear you. You stop. You press yourself flat against the wall behind you. A chunk of the wall falls off, and you catch it in your cupped palm.

You break out into a sweat, imagining the sound it would have made had it hit the ground. How the Hork-Bajir would turn, how his blades would flash in the air before tearing you apart. . . .

Wait. It's a trick you've seen a million times in movies and on TV. Would he fall for it?

Then again, do Hork-Bajir watch TV?

You grasp the stone in your fist. With your best effort, you draw back and fire the thing like a fastball, way off to the right. You hear the soft *clunk* as it falls.

The Hork-Bajir whips his horned head around and takes off after the sound, bounding like a kangaroo.

12

You run in the opposite direction. Your lungs are on fire, but you keep going. You vault over cinder blocks and debris, you swing over half-built walls. You get to your mountain bike and swing one leg over.

And then you really fly.

CHAPTER 3

You wake up the next morning feeling groggy. It was a dream, of course. A totally freaky dream that felt totally real. The worst nightmare you ever had. If you told your mom about it, she'd probably suggest counseling.

You can hear the vacuum going outside your door, and you feel better. Vacuuming is so . . . normal. How can people go on vacuuming when horrible alien slugs are invading their brains?

You peek outside the door. Your mom is vacuuming and your little sister runs out in a pink dress.

"How's this?" Lexie asks.

"Fine," Mom says, without even looking.

You remember that Lexie's birthday party is

that day. That reassures you, too. Yesterday, a six-year-old's birthday party would have been lame. Today, you think it's just about the coolest thing in the world. Because it's normal.

Your mom sees you. "Can you keep an eye on things here?" she asks. "I have to go to the store and pick up the cake."

"You're picking up the cake?" you ask. Your mom never buys a store-bought cake for birthdays. She's a city planner and works constantly, but she also has this thing about home-baked cakes.

"Emily is coming over to help, and after the party we're going to a meeting tonight," Mom tells you. "Can you baby-sit?"

"Sure," you say on the way to the kitchen. *Baby-sitting beats dodging aliens,* you think.

Not that you dodged an alien with killer blades coming out of their wrists and elbows last night. No way. It was a dream.

You chomp away on cereal, but it tastes like sawdust. You keep hearing Prince Elfangor's dying scream. You remember those dagger teeth and what they did to him. . . .

The spoon clatters in the bowl as your stomach heaves. You bend over, your face buried in your knees, and take a deep breath. That's when Marco walks into your kitchen.

"Really, you don't have to bow," he says. "A simple 'Lord Marco' will do."

"Very funny," you say. "I felt kind of dizzy for a minute."

Marco slings one leg over a kitchen chair. "It isn't every day you see an alien prince turned into McFood," he says.

"So it wasn't a bad dream," you mutter.

"Not only that, it gets worse," Marco tells you. "While you've been snoring, we've been morphing."

You stare at him. "No way."

"Way," he says, tossing his longish hair behind his shoulder. "I have been designated by our fearless leader, Jake, to recruit you. So far today, Tobias has turned into a cat, Jake into the family dog, and Cassie into a truly awesome horse."

"I don't believe you," you say.

"Yeah, I didn't want to believe it, either," Marco says, shrugging. "Considering that I'd like to remain alive long enough to get into an R-rated movie. But apparently, everything that Prince Elfa-diddle told us is true. Which means we're all in big trouble."

"You mean there might be Controllers around?" you whisper.

"Closer than you think," Marco says, reaching

for a banana. "Like Jake's brother. When I told Jake I thought Tom was a Controller, he went postal. I have the jaw to prove it." Marco rubbed his chin. "But it's the little things you notice. Tom just hasn't been acting like Tom. And he goes to this meeting called The Sharing. It sounds totally bogus, but we're all going tonight. Jake says you should come, too."

"At least it will get me out of baby-sitting," you say.

Marco peels the banana and begins to eat. Suddenly, he bends his knees and lopes around the kitchen, making monkey noises. You stare at him.

"Just kidding," he says, grinning. "I don't have a monkey morph yet. Just want you to stay on your toes."

Marco leaves, and you start thinking about what he said about Controllers. If Jake's brother Tom could be one, so could someone in your family.

What about Mom?

She bought a cake for your sister's birthday. Sure, it wouldn't sound like a big deal to most people. But you know how weird it is. She hardly noticed Lexie's party dress. Plus, didn't she say something about going to a meeting?

What if Mom is a Controller?

And if she is, how can you find out?

You decide to try your first morph and attend your sister's birthday party under cover.

You have three choices. You choose:

A fly. Go to next page.
Your sister's pet hamster. Go to page 22.
Your weird next-door neighbor's pet ferret. Go to page 25.

CHAPTER 4

It's not that easy to catch a fly. You open the window of your bedroom and wait by the sill. After about twenty-five minutes of trying to snatch one out of midair and coming up empty, you get smart. You put out a bowl of sugar water and wait. As soon as a fly lands, you snag him.

In your cupped hands, the fly buzzes furiously, but you concentrate. The fly settles into your palm. When you're done acquiring the morph, you let it go.

Marco didn't say anything about the morph being scary. But it is.

Suddenly, the ground rushes up at you. You're shrinking right out of your clothes. At the same time, your bones begin to make this funny crunching noise. It sounds like you're jumping on Styrofoam.

A leg grows out of your stomach! Then another leg! You fall facefirst on the carpet. You try to break your fall with your arms, but they are already turning transparent and papery. You hear an odd humming noise, and you realize that it's your wings, beating.

You can't see. Or rather, you can, but you see fractured images. You sense something gray and plump and interesting nearby. Thanks to the sticky pads on your feet, you walk right up a wall toward it.

Spider! You want it. You want to eat it. Chomp down on that plump, juicy body, and —

No! your mind screams. *Focus.* The spider probably has a web. And you don't want to get caught. You have a mission.

Your wings beat furiously, as if you aren't even directing them. Zoom — you're out the window, buzzing in a blur of green and blue. You head back toward the yard, where your sister's party is in full swing.

20

You land on the picnic table. The kids around you are a blur of colors. You pick up Mom's voice. She's talking to her best friend, Emily.

"Lexie wanted a store-bought ice-cream cake this year," she is saying. "I'm trying not to feel hurt. I guess she's growing up."

Emily laughs. "Kids. Mine would take a box of macaroni and cheese mix over my pasta any day."

Good news! Mom wasn't being weird. She was just doing what Lexie asked for. Maybe she's not a Controller!

Suddenly, a gust of wind sends your wings quivering. What —

Crash! A fly swatter misses you by inches! Mom is trying to swat you! You buzz up angrily, and she swats the air.

"Darn flies!" she says.

Cake! The sugary smell overwhelms you, and you can't resist. You just want to land for a moment, taste a bit . . .

But Mom swats at you again, and the gust throws you off balance. One wing dips into the frosting. You flutter it furiously, trying to get the goop off. It's making you slow and heavy, and Mom is coming with the fly swatter!

You zoom upward to escape the swatter. You buzz over the heads of the children, toward the cool shade of the tree, and —

Zap! You hit a bug zapper. You're fried!

Bad morph! Go back to page 17 and try again!

CHAPTER 5

Your hamster heart beats furiously. You're scared. You're scared of everything. Everything is bigger. Everything wants to eat you. You hide behind what, as a human, you'd consider a large hedge. But it's only a leaf of a geranium.

Morphing Hamlet, Lexie's hamster, was a weird experience. It was like being put through a meat grinder, minus the pain. Not that you've ever been put through a meat grinder. But try hearing your bones crunch. It's not the most pleasant experience.

But you do like the fur. You groom yourself, liking the glossy feel. But you have work to do. You creep closer to hear what Mom is saying to her friend Emily.

"I guess I should take a slice of cake to my neighbor," Mom says with a sigh. "If I don't, she'll come over and complain about the noise."

Just then, you smell danger. Your heart beats even faster, and you burrow into the dirt to hide. The ground shakes.

"Excuse me! This noise! Very loud!" your neighbor, Ms. Humphries, calls. A ferret is draped over her neck. The neighborhood kids call her the Ferret Lady.

Actually, you like ferrets. But as a hamster, you're terrified.

"Let me get you a piece of cake, Alice," your mom says. "It's Lexie's birthday."

"I can see that," Ms. Humphries sniffs. But she stays for the cake. "Hmmm. Store bought."

"Lexie wanted ice-cream cake," Mom says.

"Well, it looks delicious," Ms. Humphries says, suddenly sounding nice. "Quite a treat. Speaking of treats, perhaps you and your friend would like to come to a meeting tonight. Just neighbors and friends. Good food. Lots of fun."

A meeting! Could it be The Sharing? You take a few cautious steps out from your burrow.

"It sounds lovely," Mom says, surprised. The Ferret Lady has never issued an invitation before. All she does is complain about noise. "But we're going to a book group tonight."

24

"My meeting sounds much more fun," Ms. Humphries says. You creep forward another few inches, straining to hear. You should have picked an animal with better hearing!

"It's called —" Ms. Humphries begins.

But before she can finish, dirt flies and a paw suddenly swipes out. How could you have forgotten that when you see Ms. Humphries, her cat Gingerbread is never far behind?

Swipe, claw, chomp! You're dessert.

Bad choice. Why do you think hamsters stay in cages? Try again.

CHAPTER 6

You've always liked ferrets. And it's pretty cool being one. You can't see very well, but your hearing is quite excellent. And you feel so . . . happy. Playful as a kitten, but friendly, like a dog.

You leap up on an ottoman, twinkle across the back of a sofa. Being a ferret is fun!

It wasn't hard to get the morph. You waited until Ms. Humphries went next door to complain. She left the back door open, and it was easy to slip inside and pick up one of the sleek, furry creatures. It happily curled up next to your chest while you acquired its DNA.

You shrank rapidly, your body turning sleek and supple. You grew fur and whiskers and tiny claws. As soon as you morphed, you wanted to play with the three other pet ferrets. They were confused to see you, but they came over to sniff you, then chased you around the room.

The back door slams. Ms. Humphries stumps back in, a ferret draped across her chest. She looks at the ice-cream cake in her hand and shrugs. She dumps it into the kitchen trash can.

"Empty calories," she mutters. "Not necessary."

Is that a Controller thing to say? Or is the Ferret Lady even weirder than you thought? Everybody likes ice-cream cake!

You curl up under the sofa so that she won't notice she has one extra ferret. But she doesn't pay attention to her pets, anyway. Another ferret brushes against her legs. She doesn't pick it up, doesn't coo at it, doesn't stroke it.

Weird? Or standard operating procedure?

The phone rings. Ms. Humphries snatches it up.

"Yes."

A pause. "Yes. I'll be there. No, I won't attract attention," she says, sounding irritable. "No more than usual. This host is apparently an eccentric."

This host. She's a Controller!

You shrink back under the sofa. You hear a *creak* above you as she sits. You see her feet in thick-soled loafers. She doesn't move.

And doesn't move.

What time is it? How long have you been in the morph? You only have two hours! You watch as a shadow moves slowly across the floor. How can you get out of the house without her noticing you?

The shadow touches the toe of her shoe, and she gets up.

"Time," she mutters. She stumps around the room, and you creep forward to watch. She slips into her coat, picks up a nearby canvas tote bag.

She starts for the door and opens it. You can sneak out! You dart forward, but she suddenly spins around.

"Ferret Lady," she murmurs. "Travels with a pet all the time."

And before you can move or react, she reaches down and sweeps you up in one hand. She pops you into the tote bag! She zips it partly shut.

You can stick your nose out, but that's all. You're trapped, and the clock is ticking!

Ms. Humphries tosses the tote bag in the front seat of the car. You hit your head on the door handle. The car jerks forward. You try to work the zipper with your paws. No go.

How long do you have left? You can just barely see the car clock. Twenty minutes. Too close for comfort.

The car stops. Ms. Humphries slings you over her shoulder. You poke your nose out. You're in the beach parking lot. She's going to The Sharing meeting! At least the rest of the Animorphs will be there.

Ms. Humphries plops the bag down on the sand. She trudges off to speak to a knot of people by the volleyball net.

Ten minutes left. You wiggle your nose through the opening, thrashing your head to widen the gap. The zipper gives a bit. Not much. Not enough.

You hear Cassie's voice nearby. And then you remember that you can use thought-speak!

<CASSIE! CASSIE! IT'S ME! I'M IN FERRET MORPH!>

"What?" you hear Cassie say.

"I didn't say anything," someone replies. You realize that Cassie can't thought-speak back. And she can't talk out loud, or it will look suspicious.

29

<Cassie, I'm in a tote bag lying on the sand. I can't get out! My morph time is up. I think I'm near the volleyball net. Help!>

You hear the scrunch of the sand. You see bare brown toes. Cassie's concerned face suddenly looms in your vision.

"Is that you?" she whispers.

<It's me! Hurry!>

Cassie unzips the tote and casually tucks you under her arm. She strolls up toward the dunes.

"Almost there," she murmurs.

She climbs over the dunes and sets you down. She looks around. "Okay. Hurry!"

You don't need her to tell you. You concentrate, and you feel your legs getting longer. The fur on your skin grows patchy. Your ears grow rounder. Your tail shrinks.

Cassie wrinkles her nose. "Ewww. That's the worst morph I've seen so far."

"Sorry to disappoint you," you say, glad to feel that you have a mouth. "I haven't had much practice."

Rachel appears over the dune. "Hurry up, guys," she says in a low tone. "Jake is going to morph into his dog, Homer."

"Dogs and cats and ferrets," you say, suddenly feeling hopeless. "What a bunch of feeb

30

morphs. How are we going to fight Visser Three with those?"

Something fierce flashes in Rachel's eyes. You glimpse something you've never before seen in pretty, popular Rachel. The girl is a *warrior.*

"You've got a point," Rachel says.

CHAPTER 7

Things happen way fast after the meeting at the beach. Too fast. Jake morphs into a lizard and spies on Mr. Chapman, the assistant principal. He finds out that one of the entrances to the Yeerk pool is in your very own school. Every Yeerk has to visit the pool every three days in order to soak up Kandrona rays.

When Jake fills you in, you can't believe it. The whole thing sounds nuts to you. But since your life has suddenly turned crazy, every word rings true.

Rachel has taken your complaint about feeb morphs and run with it. The plan is to collect wild creature morphs at The Gardens. Since

Cassie's mother works there, you can get behind the scenes and try to acquire some truly fierce DNA.

That is, if you don't get caught.

You meet up with all the others at The Gardens.

"Okay," Cassie says, after you get your admission tickets. "Just stay close."

You follow her into the main building. It's been fashioned into a rain forest, with animals in their natural habitats.

Cassie leads you through an unmarked door. You stop, confused. Suddenly, you're in Industrial City. Gray walls, concrete floor. After the sights and sounds of the rain forest, the contrast makes you dizzy.

Cassie points to the doorways. "These lead to the exhibits," she explains.

You nod, but you can't quite imagine opening one and popping in to say hello to a tiger or a grizzly bear.

"How do you guys feel about gorillas?" Cassie asks.

You think she's kidding. But she hands Marco an apple, and before you know it, he's actually touched this huge gorilla called Big Jim. He acquires his DNA.

This gives you all courage somehow. One of you came close to a wild creature and survived.

"I say we head for the big exhibits," Marco says. "We need firepower."

You start to head toward the big creatures. But you hear a whirring sound. A golf cart is headed your way. A security guard!

"Split up!" Cassie hisses. She takes off with Tobias and Rachel. Jake and Marco are already running.

You spin around and run back the way you came. You hear the golf cart behind you, and you fake left and go right. The corridors are a maze, but this helps you. Before too long, you've lost the guard.

Now what? You wish Cassie were here to tell you what is behind the doors. You open one cautiously.

At first, all you see are treetops. The door opens out onto a little ledge, concealed by leaves. It is high above the habitat of the animal, whatever that animal is. You peer down. Something moves at your level and you jump back in alarm.

A giraffe is almost eye-level with you. It turns velvety brown eyes at you and blinks long eyelashes.

34

"Hey there," you say softly. You shake the tree branch a little. Somewhere you've read that giraffes feed on treetops. You don't think they attack humans — you hope.

The giraffe takes a delicate step toward you. It passes by you, so close you can smell the dusky fur. You put out a tentative hand and touch its flank.

The giraffe stops moving. So this is it, this is the trance. So strange that you can put such a large, strong creature to sleep. You close your eyes and concentrate.

When you're done, you pat the giraffe gently. "Thanks," you say.

You slip back inside the corridor. That encounter went so well that it gives you confidence. You continue down a sloping ramp. When you come to the next door, you open it and slip inside.

You're in a savannah. Dry trees, sand. Hot, but a dry heat. You don't see the animal at first. You hear it.

ERRRR-UP! EURRR-UP! RRR-UP!

The cry raises the hair on the back of your neck. It is close to human. The animal is wavering on long front legs. The fur is sandy-colored and coarse. You don't think you've ever seen an uglier animal.

"She should be down by now," a voice says. Quickly, you crouch down behind some food bins as the door opens.

Two white-jacketed workers come in. "Takes a few minutes," the other one says. "We better wait until she's completely out."

"Are you kidding? I wouldn't go near a hyena otherwise," the other man says. He peers into the enclosure. "She's down."

"Okay, let's go. The vet's waiting. Oh, darn. I left the stretcher by the elevator."

"Well, I'm not staying here alone."

The two workers exit. You creep toward the sleeping hyena. Just as you approach, it opens one eye. The look is deadly, like a shark's. As if your only worth is for food.

It's too late to run back now. Instead, you gather your courage and brush your hand along the creature's side.

The eye closes. Your touch, combined with the tranquilizers, has made the hyena pass out. You concentrate. As soon as you're done, you run away. Fast.

When you close the door behind you, the white-jacketed workers are heading toward you with a stretcher.

"Hey!" one of them calls.

36

"Stop!" the other one says. They toss aside the stretcher.

They start to run toward you. You could wait and think of a story. But it seems easier just to run.

CHAPTER 8

You sprint around a corner — straight into a security guard.

"Whoa," he says. Two strong hands grip your arms. "Where are you going?"

The workers come up behind you. They're both out of breath. "Tried to break into the hyena habitat," one of them says, gasping.

The grip tightens. "So what's your name, kid?"

You think about telling the truth. Well, not the whole truth. But at least saying that you know Cassie's mom. The only trouble is, that might get Cassie in trouble. And it could bring too much attention to the others. So you say nothing.

He frowns. "We got reports of vandals in the park. Come along with me."

He marches you down the corridor into a small waiting room. There are two policemen there.

Great. Just what you need.

"I know you were called about a disturbance by the snack bar," the security guard says. "But No Name here was caught sneaking into the animal habitats."

The taller policeman sighs. Obviously, he doesn't want the burden of some kid. "Let's move," he says.

They keep you between them as they march you outside to a loading area behind the snack bar. A police van is parked there. On the side of the van are the words K-9 UNIT.

"Strange thing, for a kid to be sneaking into animal cages," one of the policemen says.

"They aren't cages," the other one says. "They're habitats."

"Whatever. Sit here." The taller policeman puts a hand on your shoulder and shoves you down on a bench. "And don't think about moving. Princie and Gale won't take it too kindly."

Two German shepherds bound out of the police van and sit in front of you. One of the dogs bares its teeth.

"Stay," the policemen says, and moves off to go talk on the van radio.

You've got to get away. In just a few hours, you're supposed to meet the others at school to invade the Yeerk pool. Your only choice is a morph. But what's the best way to get away from the cops?

You have to make a choice fast, while their backs are turned. You choose:

A hyena. Go to next page.
A K-9 police dog. Go to page 43.
A giraffe. Go to page 49.

CHAPTER 9

The hyena morph roars to life — a creature bound by one instinct: To kill.

The K-9 dogs take off. They are just a streak of fur. You watch them, considering the chase. But you smell better prey.

"What the —" The policeman turns, sees you, and leaps into the van. Locks the door and reaches for a gun.

You note this, but you don't care. It just doesn't interest you. You lope away, down the path toward the snack bar. People scatter, small prey that you consider. But you smell something better.

The primitive urge to have meat is so strong that you can't fight it. You forget your name and who you are. You pick up the pace as the scent of prey grows stronger.

Stop! Your mind screams the word. *You're human! You don't kill!*

But the hyena is ruthless and fearless, and doesn't stop.

You hear a loud noise. A siren. People are screaming. Workers are rushing toward you, then stopping. One of them has a net.

You hunker down. You're cornered now. You'll have to go for the closest prey.

Small prey. Light hair grows out of the head. One of the species's young. She wanders away from her mother. Good.

It's a child! It's a little girl! No!

You can't fight it! You feel the hyena's killing instinct, and you struggle. The workers are closing in with the net. One of them carries a tranquilizer gun. He is trying to get clear to aim.

The prey toddles toward you. The mother screams. You feel the short hind legs of the hyena contract. The muscles tense. The powerful jaw opens and you let out that inhuman cry. ERRRR-UP!

It silences everyone. They all fear you. You own this place. This prey is yours.

No!

With a last, desperate struggle, you take over

42

the hyena instinct. You turn toward the worker with the gun.

You feel the burning sensation, and immediately, your legs feel heavy. Slowly, you slump to the ground.

Sting! You're knocked out. When you awake, you will have to deal with the horror of being permanently stuck in hyena morph, a creature without mercy, a killing machine.

You couldn't control the hyena instinct in time. Bad morph!

CHAPTER 10

You reach out and touch the K-9 dog Princie's coat. The dog closes his eyes. You concentrate.

The police have their backs to you. It's now or never. There's that strange sensation again, of bones crunching, things growing that shouldn't be growing. You touch your ears and feel fur. You suddenly drop down on all fours and notice that you have paws instead of hands and feet.

And the smell! You smell everything! Food! People! Animals! It's overwhelming at first. The other dogs cock their heads and look at you curiously. The one called Princie smells you and howls. After all, she's smelling herself.

The two policemen look over.

44

"Hey, Seidel," the taller one says. "Thought you only brought two dogs."

"Must have loaded a third — hey! The kid is missing!"

They rush over. You stand alert, tail twitching, like the other dogs. You're not just a dog. You're a cop. You have discipline.

It's a good morph, you tell yourself. In a minute, they'll give up on a harmless kid who stuck a toe in the wrong habitat. Big deal. It's not like you're a big bad criminal. They'll load you into the van, take you back to the station, and you can take off from there.

"This isn't good, Finley," Seidel says.

"We're supposed to be on alert," Finley answers, frowning. "Especially for kids."

Especially for kids?

"Wait, here's a shoe." One of them has spied your sneaker! "The dogs can track the kid."

He holds the sneaker under your nose. Scent roars in. *Your* scent. The other dogs smell, then strain at the leashes.

"We'll keep the one off-line, see what happens," Finley says.

The two dogs take off, and you follow, your nose to the ground, then in the air. Incredible. You can smell yourself. You can follow the air currents, know where you walked and stopped.

The dogs follow your trail to the admission booth. They circle, and you do, too. Of course you know which way you went. You go in the opposite direction, but the other two take off down the sidewalk. Darn!

You bound up behind them while the two cops hold the two leashes. Why didn't you walk on the sidewalk? That would have confused the scent. Instead, you had stuck to the grassy part near the curb. The dog can smell your trail easily.

"They've picked it up," Seidel says. He sounds relieved. More relieved than he should sound, since he's only tracking a kid.

"Chapman says at least one of the kids infiltrated The Sharing meeting," Finley says.

The policemen are Controllers!

And they'll follow your scent straight to your house. To your family.

"I reported that kid who was hanging around the dunes," Seidel answers. "The others are going to pick her up. It won't be long before she's one of us."

Cassie. She was the one who'd hung out on the dunes, watching over Jake in his dog morph. Cassie was in danger! You have to warn her. Warn the others.

The other dogs lose your scent. You almost lose it yourself. You're in a more trafficked area of town now, near the Civic Center. Earlier, you had stopped at the center garage to leave a note on your mom's car. You said you'd be late for dinner.

Even later than you'd thought.

You hurry past the garage, but the other dogs suddenly pick up your scent. They race into the garage. The cops follow, running after them.

"This isn't good!" Seidel says in a low voice. You pick up his words easily with your dog hearing.

"Visser Three won't like it," Finley says in a worried tone.

"So we won't tell him."

The dogs lose the scent amid the oil stains and gasoline. They circle around, confused. But any minute they could find your mom's car. The note you left still might be tucked under the windshield wiper. It wouldn't take the cops long to figure out who you are. This is your only chance.

You leap forward, barking, as if you've picked up the scent. You charge out of the garage. The other dogs follow. You know that you can't lead them completely astray, so you follow the route back to your neighborhood.

You run flat out now, so that the others have

trouble keeping up with you. But you make sure they keep you in sight.

You get to the Ferret Lady's house and bark furiously outside. You circle the house and find the pet door. You nose it open and bound inside.

The cops catch up and pound on the door. The Ferret Lady answers it. But already, you've caused a commotion. The ferrets are running crazily over the furniture. The cat is hissing and spitting. The other dogs add to the chaos.

"What is it?" the Ferret Lady shouts over the din.

"We're chasing a kid!" The cops try to describe you.

"Sounds like every kid in this neighborhood," the Ferret Lady sniffs. "I don't care if Visser Three himself asks me, I'll say the same."

So far, so good. You've confused them. Under cover of the chaos, you sneak out the pet door again. You bound next door. You remember leaving a sweatshirt outside after gardening chores this morning. You grab it in your mouth and race off.

You take that sweatshirt all over the neighborhood, rubbing it against trees and sidewalks and grass. Soon, you see the cops and the K-9 dogs again. The dogs are barking, running from place to place while the cops strain to hold on to the leashes.

You keep hidden and watch the cops get thoroughly confused. They give up, and you trot back home. Time is almost up.

You morph back into human form in your garage. You hurry inside to call Cassie. But everyone has left already. If you rush to the school now, you could blow their cover.

There's got to be another way.

*Good morph choice! You deserve to proceed.
Turn to page 51.*

CHAPTER 11

The giraffe morph is the strangest ever. Your legs suddenly shoot up, your bones extending so far you think they'll crack. Your neck lengthens, and you think your head will fall right off. Then your skin becomes leathery and spotted. That's kind of cool.

You like being a giraffe. You can see over everyone's heads. And boy, do your senses get a jolt. Suddenly, you can really smell for the first time. It's as though you can smell a color. You smell green, and you picture the tender leaves of the tree nearby. A good snack, you think. But it's easy to deflect the giraffe mind. You've got to get out of here.

And boy, can you *see.* Your vision is clearer

50

and sharper, and you spot an employee's exit over the trees. All you have to do is turn right at the corner of the path and keep going. You move forward delicately, like a dancer.

"Hey! It's a giraffe!"

People point at you. Oops. You kind of forgot about them down there. They seem puny, and they aren't predators. But you know that animal handlers will be coming for you with tranquilizer guns.

You quicken your pace. A giraffe can really move if it has to. But you see them, running full tilt toward you. Two of them have tranquilizer guns.

You leap over a wall. It's so easy, since your legs are so long! You find yourself in a savannah habitat. That's good. You start across, hoping to make it to the other wall. If you can get over it, the exit is just steps away.

Then, you hear the roar. You've leaped into the lion's den. Both your giraffe instincts and a book you vaguely remember called *Those Amazing Animals of Africa* suddenly remind you that lions are the main predators of giraffes.

A full-grown male lion springs.

Bad morph! You just turned into a tasty lunch. Return to page 39 and choose again.

CHAPTER 12

It's getting late, and you're freaked. Cassie is in danger. Should you head over to school to try to hook up with the others? You can't stay here while the other Animorphs put their lives on the line.

There's a suspicion that's been nagging at you. During the chase, the policemen looked very nervous at the parking garage. They muttered about Visser Three. What if something strange is going on there?

It's only a little bit out of your way, so you decide to investigate the garage before heading to school. The garage is used during the day for city government workers. Right now, it's pretty deserted except for a security guard. You duck behind a car and wait until he heads down the ramp toward the entrance.

You're about to explore when you see the guard wave in a large black van with tinted windows. Curious, you watch as the van heads up the ramp.

Instead of parking, the van pulls up directly in front of the elevators. A group of people get out. You recognize Jake's brother, Tom. Controllers!

Someone pushes a button to summon the elevator. You know you have to follow the group, but you can't stay in human form. Tom would recognize you. You have to try a morph. But what should you choose?

You have to make a decision fast. You choose:

To use your ferret morph. Go to next page.

To use your K-9 German shepherd morph. Go to page 65.

CHAPTER 13

You are concealed in a dark corner of the garage. You feel the ground rush up at you as your bones compress. Hair grows on your hands, on your face. Your nose twitches. Your body becomes sleek, and the ferret mind urges you to play. There are so many things to investigate in the garage! Wonderful smells, things to eat.

You wrench your ferret brain under control. Keeping to the wall, you get close to the group. The elevator dings, and the first group crowds on. You slink closer.

Do you dare risk boarding the elevator? The lights on the elevator are bright, and you'll probably be noticed. Normally, humans would scream if they saw a furry creature in a small space

54

with them. But you have a feeling Controllers wouldn't care.

And besides, you have no choice.

You slink in between the legs of the Controllers and head for the corner. The doors close.

"We have company," one of the Controllers says. They all look down.

"It's not a cat," someone says.

"It's not a dog," someone else observes.

The Controller who seems to be in charge turns and gives you a dismissive glance. "Catch it. I'll throw it down the shaft."

Busted! You can't react, or they'll suspect something.

"Wait," Tom says. "I've seen that animal. It's a ferret. Belongs to Humphries. Maybe we shouldn't touch it. Chapman said to take no chances."

"All right." The other Controller turns back, already bored with the conversation.

You're safe — for now.

The elevator indicator lights up the sublevel floor. It's as far down as the parking garage goes. But the Controller hits a series of buttons, and the elevator doesn't stop. It keeps going down!

The door opens onto a room that seems carved out of dirt and rock. Sheetrock is nailed up against the walls. You slink out of the elevator and follow the group into a concealed door that leads to an iron staircase.

You go down, down, down. Your eyes adjust to the light, and your nose picks up the smell of dampness. You hear something, a comforting sound that reassures you for a moment. Like waves against a shore.

But then you hear the screams. Human cries of anguish. Suffering. And you pick up a horrifyingly familiar smell. Taxxons.

You don't want to see what's ahead. You don't want to move. Dread fills you. It's so much more enormous than being afraid of a test, or the dentist.

You've only hesitated a moment, but the Controllers have disappeared around a turning. You dart forward.

The first thing you get hit with is how huge the space is. It's maybe three times the size of the mall. And it's all completely open, and carved out of rock and earth. There are still enormous pieces of earthmoving equipment down there, as though the space is constantly being expanded. You notice other staircases winding up and disappearing. There must be secret entrances all over town! The Yeerks are much more numerous than any of you imagined.

Then you notice the cages. They are filled

with humans and Hork-Bajir. Women, children, men. Some of them are screaming. Some of them just sit numbly. Taxxons and Hork-Bajir patrol outside the cages. Occasionally, one of the Hork-Bajir lashes out with a tail blade and rattles the cage. The humans shrink back, and the Yeerk-controlled Hork-Bajir let out these huffing sounds that must be laughter.

As you watch, one of the Hork-Bajir opens a cage and leads out a woman. She struggles, and the Hork-Bajir casually holds a bladed wrist to her throat. You have no doubt he would slash her in a second. The Hork-Bajir leads her onto a pier. It goes out over a pool that looks as though it's filled with moving sludge. He forces her head under the surface. When he jerks her head back up, you see a gray, slimy thing finish slithering inside her ear. The woman doesn't struggle anymore.

And then you see Tom again. His head is bent over the pool. The same slimy thing slides out of his ear.

Immediately, he begins to scream. You can't hear the words, but you can imagine. The Hork-Bajir puts a blade to his throat. It takes three of them to get him to a cage and throw him inside.

You feel sick. Sick to your bones. You can't fight this. You should turn around and go back up while you can. Wait to fight another day.

Because it's hopeless. You didn't think it was possible. But you want to give up.

Then you see Cassie. She's being held with the other humans. Waiting for a Yeerk slime to invade her brain. Guarding her are two Hork-Bajir and a Taxxon.

It's still hopeless. But rage fills you and sends your blood pounding, and you're ready to fight.

CHAPTER 14

Y‌ou scamper down the steps. No one notices you as you dart across the floor. You look like a mole, or another creature of the underground. A breeze tickles your fur and whiskers.

A breeze? Down here?

You look up. A hawk has just flown over your head. It circles the air above Cassie.

<Tobias? Is that you?>

<Who is it?>

<It's me! I'm a ferret again!>

<Cool,> Tobias answers. <We need all the help we can get. The others are about twenty feet behind you. We have to save Cassie!>

<Keep an eye on her. I'll be back.>

You scurry across the floor toward the others.

<Hey, it's me!> you call in thought-speak. <Look down.>

Marco almost jumps to the ceiling. "Why did you have to pick a rat?" he whispers.

<I'm not a rat, I'm a ferret. I'm closer to a cat or dog than a rodent. I like humans. I don't bite.>

"Great," Marco mutters. "A rodent who pretends to be a dog. Just what we need."

<You know, I can always make an exception with the biting thing,> you add.

Jake bends down to speak to you. "If I were you, I'd morph back to human. You might need a better morph than ferret. This place is crawling with Taxxons and Hork-Bajir."

<All right,> you say. <But Jake, I saw Tom! He's here! In a cage!>

"I saw him," Jake says tersely. His face tells you everything. You can't imagine how awful it must be to see your brother like that.

You scurry behind a storage shed. Quickly, you morph back to human.

Rachel pokes her head around the shed. "You'd better stay here. You need to gather your strength if you're going to morph again. We'll come back when it's time."

You lean against the storage shed and close

your eyes. You concentrate on slow breathing, gathering your strength for the next morph.

It's not long before the others return. But they've been spotted.

"What are you doing back there?"

It's a human-Controller! Standing next to him is a Hork-Bajir, blade arms at the ready. A Taxxon stands on the other side, his spidery legs twitching, red Jell-O eyes glowing.

Suddenly, you notice someone behind the guards. Rachel. Only it's Rachel with a long, long nose. A trunk. She's morphing into an elephant! A braying noise fills the air as Rachel feels the elephant's power.

She impales a Hork-Bajir on one tusk and steps on a Taxxon as though it were a spider. The human-Controller runs away.

"Let's morph!" Jake cries.

You look over at Cassie. She's almost at the end of the pier. That gives you an extra burst of strength. You concentrate hard. You feel something grow out of the back of you. A tail. Your ears get round and your head gets big. Your teeth sharpen into deadly instruments of terror.

You're a fierce, hungry, and very angry hyena. And you have no fear.

You start toward Cassie, but a Taxxon gets in

your way. No problem. You rip into him with your teeth. He tries to bite you back, but you are such an efficient killing machine that he is dead before he registers the pain.

Marco is now Big Jim, a huge gorilla. Rachel is trumpeting a fierce call as she mows down another Hork-Bajir. In tiger morph, Jake springs at a Taxxon.

You *own* this place.

Marco tosses another Hork-Bajir in the air like a doll. The rest scatter. So they *are* afraid of something.

Marco is the only one with dexterity, so he heads for the cages to unlock them. Jake is already bounding toward Cassie. You start forward to help, but a Hork-Bajir heads for you. He swipes at you with an elbow blade.

You spring. You tear at his flesh, then jump away. You strike again, this time for the vulnerable fleshy part near his head. Wounded, you expect him to fall back. But instead, he springs forward, his elbow and wrist blades flashing. Rachel raises a foot and stomps.

<Thanks,> you tell her.

<Another puny Hork-Bajir bites the dust,> Rachel says. She sounds positively bloodthirsty.

Tobias swoops down and claws at the eyes of

the Hork-Bajir who is holding Cassie. She breaks away and runs.

<Morph!> you yell along with Jake. <Now!>

Even as you watch, Cassie's hair grows into a beautiful mane. It streams out behind her as her legs extend, and she goes down on all fours. It is amazing to see.

<I say we follow Cassie and get out of here,> Rachel says.

<I'm right behind you,> you say.

The people Marco have released are panicking, running toward the stairs. Hork-Bajir and Taxxons try to round them up. You slip through them, running hard.

Cassie and Jake leap over surprised Taxxons. You remember that Hork-Bajir aren't great on strategy, so you fake left and then go right, sailing over a long pair of wrist blades that try to slash you at the last minute.

You gain the stairs. Balls of flame explode over your head. You leap over a Taxxon who is aiming a Dracon beam at you. Straight into the path of Visser Three in his Andalite form.

The horrid, evil voice fills your head. <Well, if it isn't a bunch of renegade Andalites.>

He begins to morph into a creature tall as a building. Eight legs. Eight arms. And eight heads. You can feel that even the hyena inside you feels doubt. You can't take on this creature.

<You can't escape!> Visser Three cries.

"You filthy creep!" It's Tom. Jake's brother launches himself at Visser Three.

<NO!> Jake cries. He springs at the huge creature that is Visser Three, straight toward the eyes. He claws at the face. Visser Three howls in pain.

Fireballs explode. One almost gets Jake. Tom falls off the stairs.

<Jake, run!> Cassie cries urgently.

With a howl of anguish, Jake turns and heads up the stairs. Rachel begins to demorph as she climbs so she can fit in the stairway.

<You can't run!> Visser Three cries.

Oh yes, you can. The stairway narrows. Visser Three hadn't counted on your making it that far. In his huge morph, he can't make it upstairs.

You run and you run. You break through the janitor's door and back into school. You keep on running until you're outside, in the safety of the trees. And then you all morph back.

You're safe. For now.

You look at your friends and see the same exhaustion on their faces. Even Marco can't come up with a joke. Cassie puts her hand over Jake's.

64

Rachel stares back at the school building, her eyes blazing. Tobias flies closer and perches on her shoulder.

You know that more terror lies ahead. You know that safety is now an illusion. You will never feel truly safe again.

Excellent morph! Turn to page 69 for your next Animorph adventure.

CHAPTER 15

Your ears grow straight up. Fur sprouts on your face and hands. You fall onto all fours. Suddenly, you smell everything. Oil. Car exhaust. Human smells. Mice. And over in the corner, a paper bag with a peanut butter sandwich.

You trot over to the group waiting for the elevator. You stay behind them. When the elevator comes, you leap on just as the doors close.

You make it down in the elevator without anyone really caring. The elevator hits the sublevel, but a Controller pushes a series of buttons and it keeps going down. When it stops, everyone files out. The last Controller pushes you back into the elevator.

66

"Beat it, bub," he says.

The doors close, but you leap up against the panel and hit the STOP button with your paw. You wait. After a few minutes, you butt the DOOR OPEN button with your head.

The doors open onto a small room. You see the last Controller just disappearing through the hidden door. You bound over and stick your body half-in to keep it open, then slip inside.

But the Controller sees you.

"Hey!" He looks at you, suspicious now. You take a step backward. You bare your teeth and try a growl. He drops back, but another Controller steps up the stairs.

It's Finley, the policeman!

"Grab him!" he cries.

The other Controller reaches for your collar, and you sink your teeth into his hand. With a howl, he steps back. But Finley springs forward and grabs your collar. He half drags you down the steps.

You see a huge cavern patrolled by Taxxons and Hork-Bajir. There are humans in cages. The screams seem more terrible to your sensitive ears.

Finley hands you over to a Hork-Bajir. "Keep it. Something's weird about this dog."

The Hork-Bajir fastens a leash from a chain. He attaches it to a piece of heavy machinery. Then he holds one of his blades to your throat. The message is clear. Move, and you die.

You decide to sit still. All you can do is watch.

Watch as Jake, Rachel, and Marco morph into fierce animals. Watch as they attack. Watch as the Hork-Bajir and Taxxons fight them. Watch as Visser Three morphs into a horrible creature with eight heads, tall as a two-story building.

You want to cheer when the others get away, running up the staircase. You want to cry when you see Jake's brother Tom tossed back into the cage.

Then one of Visser Three's eight heads swivels. His eyes fix on you.

<What have we here?> His voice is like the sludge in the Yeerk pool. Thick and evil.

You put your head into your paws, like a dog might. Your tail is stiff and straight.

<Welcome, Andalite,> Visser Three says. <Your friends didn't want to stay for dinner. How kind of you to remain.>

He laughs, and you see his teeth glinting. They are sharp and pointed like daggers. He

68

raises one of his many hands, and a fireball zooms past you.

<Time to get roasted,> Visser Three says. His hand lifts again, and he sends another fireball your way. This one hits its mark.

SIZZLE! You're dead.

Bad morph choice. You took the chance you might be recognized. You lost.

CHAPTER 16

"Pizza for dinner?" your mom says.

"Awesome," you say.

It's a Saturday afternoon. You just returned from the mall. Sometimes, you just need an ordinary day.

You've been on plenty of missions with the Animorphs. Your close calls have given you nightmares. You are living in a world with new rules. Sometimes, you think you'll go crazy. Sometimes you *want* to go crazy. Living with stark terror every day will do that to you.

So whenever you can, you try to do something normal. As much as morphing into an osprey might be fun, it isn't normal. Not by a long shot.

So when you called Jake that morning to ask

if anything was up, he just sighed. "I say we take a day off from saving the world," he said.

The smell of green peppers fills the kitchen. You watch your mom chop. She makes her own pizza, and it's the best in town.

"Can we have sausage on it?" you ask.

Mom grins. "Sure. It's Saturday. Let's live a little."

You reach into the refrigerator for a soda, and —

FLASH! The heat presses against your skin. You hear the call of birds and insects.

"Where did you guys go?" Rachel asks.

"And where are we?" Cassie wonders.

"And why don't I have shoes?" Marco asks. FLASH!

"— and a nice green salad," Mom finishes. "I have to sneak something healthy in there."

Your hand is cold. You look at the sweat beading up on the can. *Whoa. What was that about?* It was SO *real.* The heat had been just as intense as the cold in your fingers right now.

"Can you hand me that garlic?" Mom asks.

You nod and reach for a garlic bulb in a bowl on the counter. You hand it to Mom, and —

FLASH!

"Really, a monkey morph?" Marco says, lifting an eyebrow. "Listen, I've been a gorilla. That would be quite a demotion, don't you think?"

"Marco, I'm just wondering," Rachel says, her hands on her hips. "Do you *always* have to make things difficult? Is it like, your hobby?"

"It's my *life*," Marco says.

FLASH!

"— would you do me a favor and pick some basil off the plant?" Mom asks. "Sweetie? Are you okay?"

"I'm okay," you say. But you're not. Something is really, truly wrong. And you have to find out what.

"It sounds like a *Sario Rip*," Jake says worriedly.

You've ridden as fast as you can on your bike to Jake's house. You only have a half hour before dinner. Ax is there, too, and he looks just as worried as Jake. He'd been eating his very first licorice whip, and he'd been really enjoying it. But he stopped when you blurted out your story.

"Not again," he says. "No, not again, Prince Jake. This is not good."

"What's a *Sario Rip*?" you ask.

"Are you sure it was a jungle?" Jake asks, instead of answering you. "Or was it a rain forest?"

"Like I can tell the difference?" you ask. You're starting to feel impatient.

Jake turns to Ax. "But I reversed the *rip*. How can this happen?"

Ax shrugs and begins to chew on the end of the licorice. "I don't know. When they taught about *Sario Rips* in class, I was —"

"Not paying attention," Jake finishes impatiently. "I know."

"Young Andalite females can do that," Ax says. He slurps up another inch of licorice. "This tastes red. R-r-rred. Tastes red. Red-duh."

"Cherry," Jake says absently. "It's cherry-flavored."

"Will somebody please fill me in?" you demand.

"A *Sario Rip* is like a hole in space-time," Jake explains. "We've all experienced it, except I'm the only one who remembers it. That's because I died back there, but not in this time, so I was able to come back."

"Oh, thanks," you say. "That clears it up. Totally."

"The thing is that Ax said, you need some sort of huge explosion to blow you back," Jake says worriedly. "I guess maybe it hasn't happened yet."

"Terrific," you say. "Something to look forward to besides pizza. Nuclear annihilation."

"Unless we're in a *rip* right now," Ax puts in. "A *rip* within a *rip*."

Jake frowns. "What does that mean?"

Ax shrugs. It could be his first shrug, because he looks surprised at the motion. He does it again for practice. "I do not know. I am just guessing. Want some licorice?" He holds a piece out to you, and —

FLASH!

CHAPTER 17

The trees soar above your heads. The leaves make a canopy so dense it blocks out the sky. The heat presses against your skin.

"Whoa!" Jake cries. "What's going on?"

"Wait," you say. "You mean you *know* you're here? With me?"

"It's the same place," Jake says, spinning around. "Hang on."

He darts through the trees, and you and Ax follow. You stop abruptly when Jake does, bumping into him. In a small clearing is a Bug fighter. It is scorched and trashed, as though it had crash-landed.

"This is totally freaked," Jake whispers.

"I'll say," a voice says. It's Rachel, who steps

through the trees, Cassie and Marco at her side. "Where did you guys go?"

"And where are we?" Cassie asks.

"And why don't I have shoes?" Marco asks glumly, staring at his bare feet.

<I've been circling above, but all I see is a green canopy of trees,> Tobias says in thought-speak. He swoops down and lands on a tree trunk. <I'd say we're in a rain forest. I can try to see if there's a city or a village nearby.>

"There's no city," Jake mutters.

"Pray tell, how do you know, O Fearless Leader?" Marco asks.

"I just do," Jake says. He frowns. "The first thing we have to do is take the onboard navigating computer. Visser Three will be coming back for the Bug fighter."

"How do you know this stuff?" Cassie asks. "The last thing I remember I was on the Bug ship. We were shooting Dracon beams at Visser Three."

"It's a *Sario Rip,*" Jake says. Quickly, he summarizes what has happened.

"So how do we get back?" Cassie asks. You can tell she's trying not to look scared.

"I'm not sure," Jake admits. "Last time, I had to die. I don't especially want to do that again."

"Are you all thinking what I am thinking?" Ax asks suddenly.

Marco rolls his eyes. "What are the odds of that?"

"Think about it, Prince Jake," Ax continues. "You have been given a second chance. Last time, you made mistakes. What I mean to say is, you made good decisions, but things went wrong."

"Thanks for trying to make me feel better, Ax, but you were right the first time," Jake says wryly. "We walked right into Visser Three's trap."

"But this time, we will not walk into the trap," Ax points out. "We know what is *wrong* to do. Now we must do what is *right* to do."

"You're right, Ax!" Jake says excitedly. "We've been given a second chance! And the first thing we should do is *not* take the onboard computer. Can you just disable it instead? Make it look like it happened in the crash, but be sure that they can fix it. That will slow them down while we follow through on a plan."

"I can do this, Prince Jake," Ax says, nodding. He takes off for the Bug fighter.

"What plan?" Marco asks. "Call me crazy, but I have a feeling I'm not going to like this."

"It's simple," Jake says. "We're going to sneak onboard the Blade ship —"

"Already, I don't like it," Marco interrupts, groaning.

"— and destroy Visser Three," Jake says grimly. "Then we'll re-create the *rip* and get back to our own time."

"Sounds like a good plan," Rachel agrees. "Especially the 'destroy Visser Three' part."

"Of course *you'd* think so," Marco says. "What do you need morphing ability for? You're already an animal."

"The question is, what should we morph?" Cassie asks. "We have to get through the rain forest, and we're barefoot. How about monkeys?"

"Really, a monkey morph?" Marco says, lifting an eyebrow. "Listen, I've been a gorilla. That would be quite a demotion, don't you think?"

"Marco, I'm just wondering," Rachel says, her hands on her hips. "Do you *always* have to make things difficult? Is it like, your hobby?"

"It's his life," you say.

Marco gives you a strange look. "I was going to say that."

"I know," you say.

"Come on, guys," Jake says. "We have decisions to make. We have to acquire morphs that will help us cope with the rain forest. But we also need morphs that will help us sneak aboard the Blade ship."

"And we might need the help of that tribe you met last time," Ax says as he reappears. "You said they were pretty helpful against the Hork-Bajir."

"What about using an ant morph again?" you suggest. You point to a tree. "I read about those ants. They're called parasol ants. They can climb hundreds of feet. And we'd be so small we'd sneak onto the Bug fighter with no problem."

"That's true," Cassie says reluctantly.

"No way I'm being an ant again," Marco says, shuddering. "That was the worst."

You all begin to argue about what morphs to acquire. But you're running out of time. You might only have time for one morph.

You choose:

A monkey. Go to next page.
A parrot. Go to page 83.
A parasol ant. Go to page 89.

CHAPTER 18

You'd felt out of place in the rain forest. First of all, the bugs alone are enough to send you screaming toward the horizon. If there'd been a horizon.

But once you morph a monkey, you discover that the vines you thought of as choking off air and light are . . . well, like monkey bars.

Which gives you a chance to use what must be the coolest tail in the universe.

<Cooler than mine?> Ax asks.

<Sorry, Ax-man,> Marco tells him. <Way cooler.>

You all scamper up trees, grab vines, and swing. You reach the high branches and just let yourself go, out into space, and you catch a branch with your tail.

KIKKKI CHACCHACH KI KI KI!

You swing past Rachel, grab a branch with your hand, hang in midair a minute, launch yourself toward a vine. You bare your teeth at her.

KIKI CHEE CHEE!

<I can do that!> Rachel calls. She grabs the same vine, swings over, and lands on your branch. She bares her teeth at you, too.

<Uh, guys? Can you stop playing for a minute?> Tobias sits on a branch near you. He sounds almost sulky. <Shouldn't we be following through on our plan?>

Marco swings back and forth on a vine. <Who needs a plan? Forget Visser Three. This is like being a six-year-old forever, only with no school.>

<That is *kidding,* correct?> Ax asks.

<It's kidding,> Jake tells him.

<That's what you think,> Marco says.

<Shhh,> Cassie says. <I think I hear something.>

Then you hear it, too. Some creatures are crashing through the underbrush.

<I bet that's our search party,> Jake says.

<There's a human-Controller leading them,> Tobias says from his high branch. <I'll get closer.> With a flap of wings, Tobias takes off.

<A human can tell them what creatures don't belong here,> Jake says. <Tobias, stay out of sight!>

<I just want to see how many — whoa, Dracon beam!> Tobias shouts. <I think he saw —>

<Tobias?> Rachel says frantically.

You all exchange worried glances. You take off, grabbing vines and branches and swinging through the trees. Before, it was a game. Now, it is life or death.

You see Tobias ahead. He has been caught in a net. He's been hit by a Dracon beam.

<Tobias!> Rachel cries.

<I'm singed, but okay,> he answers. <I just can't get out of this net.>

Rachel goes into action. She launches herself out into midair and grabs a vine. She swings over and lands on Tobias's branch. Using her sharp teeth, she begins to shred the net while she pulls it apart with her hands.

"That's no monkey!" the human-Controller shouts.

A Dracon beam explodes near Rachel. You need to cover her. You swing over and begin to chatter, trying to draw the Hork-Bajir's fire. You grab a vine and swing right by a Hork-Bajir. He slashes in the air after you, but you're gone.

"That one. The little one. Get him!"

82

A Dracon beam explodes near you, felling a tree in half. Before you can scamper up the next tree or grab a vine, another one explodes. This one gets you, and you fall.

Straight onto the lethal blade of a Hork-Bajir.

Oops — bad morph. Go back to page 78 and try again.

CHAPTER 19

You don't have the same wing strength as a bird of prey, but at least you can fly. The parrot morph allows you to soar just underneath the upper canopy. Your green feathers offer camouflage.

<I like this morph,> Cassie says. <I really feel like I belong here.>

<As long as Tobias doesn't eat us for lunch,> Marco says, dipping under a tree branch and then soaring upward.

<I'm sure getting a workout,> Jake says. <This isn't like being a falcon and soaring with the thermals. You really have to work.>

<Well, work it, girl,> Marco teases.

84

<How do you know I'm a girl?> Jake asks.

<Because that red tail is so adorable,> Marco answers.

Everyone laughs, and it comes out in parrot-speak. C-c-c-err-EPP-err-EPP! It feels good to laugh, even if you're doing it with a thick, curved beak.

<Pipe down, you guys,> Tobias warns. <I see them.>

Tobias has been flying ahead of the group. With his superior eyesight and wing power, he is able to see the Hork-Bajir from far away.

<They're destroying everything!> Tobias suddenly shouts. <Must have gotten bored just looking. They're slashing and burning!>

<Okay, fade back, Tobias,> Jake warns. <We'll take over.>

<They just killed a sloth and her babies,> Tobias continues. <For nothing! Those murderers!>

<*Now,* Tobias!> Jake shouts.

In another moment, you see a blur of brown feathers. Tobias drops onto a branch. <They're killing everything that moves,> he says in disbelief.

<That is what the Yeerks are best at,> Ax says quietly.

You leave Tobias behind and fly ahead. You hear the Hork-Bajir before you see them. Dracon beams sizzle. The smell of burnt things fills the air. You hear the cries of what sounds like thousands of birds, fellow creatures trying to flee.

<Guys?> It's Rachel, who has spurted ahead, her wings just a blur of motion. <I think I see something. Look down by that weird tree.>

<Gee, thanks, Rach, that really narrows it down,> Marco says.

<The one with the roots,> Rachel says impatiently.

You look down. You see nothing. Just branches and leaves. But then the leaves move, and you see a person concealed behind them. He is holding a spear. And then you see another, and another.

You've found the tribe.

<They're spying on the Hork-Bajir,> Cassie whispers. It's funny how you sometimes feel a need to whisper, even though you're talking in thought-speak.

<I have a plan,> Jake says. <Follow me and do what I do.>

He swoops down and lands on the shoulder of one of the tribe. They are men and boys, all with dark hair and alert dark eyes. They are wearing something that looks like a diaper made out of leaves.

You swoop down on another shoulder. Rachel follows. Then Cassie. Marco. Ax. Tobias flutters down and lands on a low branch.

The tribe does nothing. They don't even move a muscle. But you see every pair of eyes turn to one man. He is either your age or your grandfather's. It's hard to tell.

<Cassie,> Jake says. <You morph.>

Cassie doesn't even ask why. She flies to the center of the clearing.

You wonder why he's chosen Cassie. But as Cassie begins to morph, you understand. Cassie can control her morph so that she changes gracefully. She isn't scary. She's beautiful.

She retains her bright feathers as she grows. She changes her face first, so at first she's a bird-girl. Her tail retracts, but her feathered wings still flutter. Slowly, her feathers turn into smooth skin, starting with her feet and slowly moving up her body.

Again, the tribe doesn't move. They don't raise their spears.

"Espirito," the leader says.

<He called her a spirit,> Marco translates.

<Cassie, nod,> Jake directs.

Cassie nods. She holds out her arms as though she is gathering the tribe to her. It is a welcoming gesture. You realize she is telling them not to be afraid.

<Now draw a Hork-Bajir with a stick,> Jake tells her.

Cassie bends over and draws the Hork-Bajir in the dust. It's not a great drawing, but the Hork-Bajir are pretty distinctive.

"Diablo," the leader says.

<Devil,> Marco says.

Cassie nods.

<Now draw the Blade ship,> Jake directs. <They need to understand that we have to get aboard.>

Cassie draws the Blade ship. She points to herself and the ship. Then she points to the leader and stabs the Hork-Bajir with her stick.

The leader grins. He throws his spear.

<Cassie!> Rachel cries.

But the spear just misses Cassie and lands at her feet. Straight into the center of the Hork-Bajir drawing.

Cassie smiles. The leader smiles.

You all say CA-CA-CA-Err-EPP-Err-EPP!

Cassie needs time to recover from her morph, so you all rest in human form. With a combination of signs and pointing, Cassie has arranged

88

to meet up with the tribe again just as dusk falls.

Your parrot morph was successful. You met up with the tribe and escaped the notice of the Hork-Bajir. But you need another morph to sneak aboard the Blade ship.

You choose:

Chameleon. Turn to page 92.
Poison-arrow frog. Turn to page 110.
Jaguar. Turn to page 113.

CHAPTER 20

The parasol ant morph makes sense. Who notices an ant? You congratulate yourself on your bright idea.

Until you're an ant. The others had really warned you about this morph. They told you how hard it was to hang onto their own selves during it. The ant has no self. It is focused on solely food and enemies and getting back to the colony.

So you thought you were prepared. But the loss of self frightens you intensely. Your antennae wave in front of you, smelling for food and enemies.

90

<Stay focused, everyone,> Jake orders.

You start up a tree. That's what you're supposed to do. Got to find food.

<Let's get this over with,> Marco says. <I *hate* the ant morph.>

<I must admit, this is not a creature I would want to morph again,> Ax says.

<Hold it!> Tobias warns. <I only see five of you.>

The others tick off a roll call. You don't answer. You're halfway up the tree now. You've got to keep going.

Food is up here. You can bring food back to the colony. You smell something dead. A beetle. You will dismember it, carry pieces back.

<Guys, we have a problem,> Tobias says.

<Get a hold of yourself! You're not an ant!> Jake yells at you.

And your human mind screams to life. You don't want to dismember a beetle. A beetle leg is not your idea of good eating.

<All right,> you say shakily. <I'm back. I'm okay. But *whew*. That was a close one.>

Closer than you think. Because hanging on a tree branch over you is a sloth. And she's hungry.

She hangs onto the branch with her tail while her head swings past you. Her long tongue swoops out, and —

SLURP! You're lunch.

Not your best morph. Go back to page 78 and try again.

CHAPTER 21

First, your skin turns green.

"Are we Martians or reptiles?" Marco is just able to get out before he is unable to speak. The rest of his complaint sounds like *ack ack.*

<I love this tail!> Cassie thought-speaks.

You know what she means. A chameleon's tail is almost like a monkey's — curled and strong. You roll your eyes. One goes left, the other right. You can get a 180-degree view without turning your head.

You follow behind the others as you make your way to the perimeter of the landing site.

<Okay, remember, when you see Visser Three in the window of the Blade ship, it's only a de-

coy,> Jake says. <That's what he did in the last *Sario Rip.* So all we have to do is come to the ship from behind. And meanwhile, the tribe will cover us with a diversion.>

<If all goes as planned,> you say.

<Which it never does,> Marco adds.

<The tribe is in place,> Tobias tells you. <Visser Three is in *Lerdethak* mode. I can see the vines moving.>

Jake has told you about Visser Three's morph. The *Lerdethak* is as tall as a tree. It has hundreds of vinelike tentacles. They can strike like whips and squeeze all the breath out of you. Then the *Lerdethak* can just pop you in its cavernous mouth like Good and Plenty.

It's an experience you're happy to skip.

<It's dusk,> Cassie observes. <Time for the tribe to attack.>

Your coloring protects you as you scurry along the floor. You belong to the forest, are part of the forest. You can hear the sound of Hork-Bajir in the distance, but you are quick and agile and unafraid. You let the chameleon's instincts take over.

Because if you let your human mind start to think, it will fill up with fear. You are running toward Visser Three. Not away from him.

<The tribe is attacking!> Tobias, the lookout, tells you. <They keep melting back into the forest. The Hork-Bajir are going crazy.>

<Get onto the Blade ship, Tobias,> Jake urges while he runs. <Do it!>

You are running flat out now. A chameleon can't run very fast, not as fast as a jaguar, but you reach the burned-out clearing. The Blade ship looms ahead.

Jake goes first. Then Rachel. One by one, moving as fast as you dare, but keeping to the dark green shadows, you approach the huge, black ship. The gangway is down. You all scamper up it, then keep to the side walls of the ship.

<Tobias?> Jake asks.

<I'm here. Up high, in the rafters.>

You roll your eyes up. You can just barely make out Tobias.

<You're all changing color,> Tobias observes. <You're getting darker.>

<May I make a suggestion, Prince Jake?> Ax says. <Perhaps we should scatter. One chameleon might have wandered aboard, but not six.>

<Good point,> Jake agrees. <Let's find separate positions. We have to wait until the ship goes back to the same space position and fires its rockets. Then we should land back in our own time.>

<What about Visser Three?> Ax asks.

<When do we destroy him?> Rachel asks. <Shouldn't we pick a place to hide where we can morph into something really dangerous? We can take him by surprise.>

Jake hesitates.

<Wasn't that the plan?> Rachel asks urgently.

<I'm not sure now,> Jake says. <It might be too dangerous. Maybe we should just let Visser Three blast us back into our own time.>

<But we'll lose our chance!> Rachel argues.

<I'm with Jake,> Marco says. <If we live, we can come back and fight another day.>

<I'll go with whatever you all decide,> Cassie says.

<If I can get a word in,> Tobias says. <This ship is constantly patrolled. And the bridge is full of Taxxons. We might be able to take down Visser Three if we're incredibly lucky. But that doesn't mean we'll survive.>

<Ax?> Jake asks.

<Visser Three killed my brother. He is my sworn enemy,> Ax says. <I will meet with him someday. It may not be today. I will follow your decision, Prince Jake.>

<I wish you didn't say that,> Jake groans.

<It's this *Sario Rip* that's complicating

things,> you say. <We don't know if we'll make it back. We don't know if we're part of someone's memory. If we kill Visser Three now, in this time, what happens to us in real time?>

<This is way too confusing,> Cassie sighs.

<I need a nap,> Marco says. <And I haven't said that since I was three years old.>

<Let's hide,> Jake says finally. <We still have time to decide. Time is running out for Visser Three. He can't afford to chase that tribe around the forest any longer.>

The six of you melt behind a console. You space yourselves apart, but within thought-speaking distance.

<Leave them!> A terrible voice invades your head. If you had hands, you'd put them over your ears. When Visser Three talks in thought-speak, it feels as though your whole brain shudders.

<Leave them behind,> Visser Three continues. He is back in Andalite morph. <It is not the punishment those Andalites deserve, but it will have to be enough.>

Visser Three places himself in one of the chairs on the bridge. <Now take off, you worthless slime,> he says to the Taxxon captain.

A message crackles over the communication system. "Bug fighter ready for takeoff."

<So take off, fool!> Visser Three roars in thought-speak.

You can feel the great ship rise, but you can't see anything. You feel a burst of optimism. It feels like the first step toward home.

<Ax, keep track of the time for us,> Jake advises in private thought-speak.

<I will, Prince Jake,> Ax says. <But there is no telling when Visser Three will order the double blast. The Bug fighter and the Blade ship have to intersect those Dracon beams. Perhaps they have already agreed on a coordinate. There is no way of knowing.>

<Which means,> Rachel says, <that if we do want to attack Visser Three, we'd better do it soon.>

<All right,> Jake says. <Maybe we should —>

He is cut off by the bleating of Visser Three shouting <Now!>

The blast rocks you.

FLASH!

You're in the front quad outside school. You're wearing a sweater you haven't worn since last year. Ahead of you is the bus stop. You see Patrolman Teeter directing traffic. He retired last summer.

You turn. Rachel is back on the steps of

school. Her hair is a good four inches shorter. She touches it, frowning.

She wore it that way last year. You've gone back in time like you should have. But you've overshot your time.

You're a year too early.

"What's going on?" you say. This isn't a flashback. It's going on too long. But it doesn't feel real, either.

"Oh, man," Marco says. "Does this mean I have to go through homeroom with Ms. Pedalowski again?"

"Something's wrong," you say.

Just then, a car pulls up to the curb. A window slides down. Marco's mother waves at him.

"Hi, honey! Thought I'd give you a ride."

Next to you, Marco has gone completely still. His mother is dead. That's what everyone thinks, anyway. Only you, Jake, and Ax know that Marco's mother was taken over by the Yeerks. She is Visser Three's rival, Visser One.

100

Marco takes a step forward. He moves stiffly, like he's frozen. You can see tears in his eyes. His mom is so *alive*! A breeze lifts her heavy dark hair. Her hand rests on the open window. Her wedding ring glints in the sun.

"Come on, slowpoke!" she teases. "Have you got lead in your shoes?"

"Mom," Marco whispers.

Marco's mom swings the door open and steps out onto the curb. It is as though everything is in slow motion. You are shocked to see her alive and warm and happy.

So it takes you longer than it should to see the pit bull. It runs across the grass toward her.

Then you hear the voice that haunts your nightmares. <I will end it here!>

"Marco!" you cry. "It's Visser Three!"

Marco starts to run. But you know in a split second that you can't fight this dog. Not as a human, anyway. He is too far away. You have only seconds. You have to try a morph.

You choose:

Hyena. Go to page 101.
K-9 dog. Go to page 103.
Giraffe. Go to page 105.

CHAPTER 23

It's the fastest you've ever morphed. Maybe panic helps you. Your powerful hind legs develop first. Then, your face flattens, your teeth grow. You feel the power in your muscles. You feel the urge to make your kill.

The dog is on Marco's mother. It tears at the arm she flings up to protect her throat.

A pit bull is no match for you, a killing machine. You leap forward with the high-pitched, almost-human cry of the animal.

ERRRR-UP! EURRR-UP! RRR-UP!

Your teeth find the pit bull's leg. You chomp down and hit bone. Snarling, the pit bull turns. That exposes its neck, and you pounce. You have Visser Three in your jaws. You savor the moment.

102

What you didn't count on was Patrolman Teeter.

He has been on the school beat for ten years. He loves the kids. He protects them from bullies, stray dogs, and fast cars.

He certainly isn't going to let a hyena endanger them.

He runs up behind you and pulls his gun.

Bang! You're dead.

Bad morph. You should have thought about Patrolman Teeter. Visser Three is still alive, and you're just a dead hyena.

CHAPTER 24

A K-9 dog is highly trained for tracking. It is also trained in defense. It is a match for a pit bull.

But is it a match for a pit bull controlled by Visser Three?

The evil force of Visser Three joins with the powerful jaws and killing instinct of the pit bull. The combined force turns the animal into a creature three times as deadly.

You leap on the dog's back. You are bigger, and you use your bulk to force the dog down. You sink your teeth into the fur around his neck and pull him off Marco's mother.

The two of you roll backward. Patrolman

104

Teeter runs forward. But he won't draw his gun, not on two dogs.

All you hear are the snarls of your adversary. You smell blood and terror. The terror is yours. You realize that you are outmatched.

The pit bill's teeth rip into your throat. You can't bark. You can't speak. You try to morph back, but your life force is ebbing.

RIP — you're dead. Go back to page 100 and try again.

CHAPTER 25

You leap behind a tree to accomplish your giraffe morph. Your legs grow so rapidly that you crack your head on a branch. Your neck stretches. Your skin is patterned with tan and brown.

With a clatter of hooves, you take off toward Marco's mother. You are there in three powerful strides.

Giraffes are peaceful creatures. Patrolman Teeter is stunned to see one appear, but he doesn't go for his gun. He would never shoot a giraffe.

You turn your back to the dog to give yourself greater kicking power. He launches himself at you, but he can only reach your leg. You shake him off, you pull back your leg, and —

WHAM! You knock Visser Three into next week.

FLASH!

"— onions on it, too?" Mom asks you. She is stirring a pot of tomato sauce at the kitchen stove.

She turns when you don't answer. "Sweetie? Do you want onions on the pizza?"

"Sure," you say. "Everything. But I have to go to Jake's for a minute. I forgot my . . . home-work."

"It's Saturday."

"Yeah," you say, and run out.

"Ask him over for dinner!" your mom yells as you hop on your bike. You ride like the wind. You find Jake and Ax in the bedroom. Ax is only halfway through his licorice whip. You spill out your story.

"We were all there?" Jake asks. "And I *knew* I was in a second *Sario Rip*?"

You nod. "And when we went back in time, Marco and I both knew we were in the wrong time. Marco knew his mother was dead. Gone. Whatever."

Jake looks at Ax. "Does any of this make sense to you?"

Ax chews on the licorice and swallows. "No. Except for the motive of Visser Three. He manipulated the *Sario Rip* to go back farther in time."

"He knew it would happen?" Jake asks.

"He was trying to kill his enemy's host before it became the host," Ax explains. "You see, some hosts are better than others. Obviously, Visser One has found a host that has extraordinary abilities. I also guess that Visser Three might have known you were aboard in some kind of morphs. That was a trap. Since he thinks you are Andalites, perhaps he thought he could send you back. That way, he would be prepared that first night when my brother, Elfangor, landed. He would make sure to kill you. Or else you would not be there at all. Alter the past, alter the future. He was willing to take the risk."

Jake groans. "So I fell into another trap in the Amazon? Swell! I can't even be smart in someone else's *Sario Rip*!"

"But it turned out well, Prince Jake," Ax points out. "Visser Three was stopped by the giraffe morph. That is why the whole thing never happened. He returned to the original time of the *rip* so that he wouldn't be stopped. The good news is that Marco's mother was not killed. So Visser One is still Visser Three's enemy. Which is good for us. To have them fighting for power distracts Visser Three."

"But I don't get it," you say. "If I was in Visser Three's *rip*, why do I remember it? And why did you and Jake remember some of it back in the Amazon?"

Ax thoughtfully braids a licorice ribbon, then bites off a piece. "Muffmsx."

"Is that Andalite language?" Jake asks.

"No, it is a mouthful of licorice," Ax responds. "The answer is, I do not know. My guess is that there can be breaks in the *rip*. Like this."

He holds up a braid of licorice. Light shines through the holes. "I was not paying attention the —"

"— day *Sario Rips* were taught," you finish. "We know!"

Ax shrugs. "Someday we might figure it out. But you are alive. You saved Marco's mother. That is the important thing. We have lived to fight another day."

"Ax is right," Jake tells you. "You have to take what you can get, these days. Worry about the things you can do something about. You're alive, and so are we."

You know he's right. You have to take the moment. You're safe. You may not have killed Visser Three, but you're back in your own time. Alive.

Jake puts his hand on your shoulder. "Don't worry. There will still be more battles to fight."

You grin. "But first," you say, "there's pizza."

CHAPTER 26

The poison-arrow frogs are a good cover. With your powerful hind legs, you leap through the rain forest to the site of the Blade ship. You lurk underneath a bush, waiting for Tobias's signal.

<They've started fighting,> Tobias says. <Where are you? I can't see you.>

<To the right of the Blade ship,> you say.

<Underneath that bush with the pointy leaves,> Cassie adds.

<I still can't see you. And I can't find Visser

Three. He could be in a new morph,> Tobias says.

<Watch,> you say. You hop out a few feet into the clearing.

<Okay, got you,> Tobias says. <You'd better circle to the other side. There's Hork-Bajir in your vicinity.>

You hop back. Together with the others, you make your way around the ship. Around you, you can hear the Hork-Bajir crashing through the rain forest. Every so often, you hear the sizzle of Dracon beams.

It begins to rain. You're thirsty, and your frog brain clamors for water. You hop forward and stick out your tongue. The water feels cool. You swallow gratefully.

<The rain feels good,> you say.

<What rain?> Tobias asks.

A brownish-greenish creature suddenly detaches itself from a tree. It appears to have no bones. But at the end of its five arms are sprinklerlike holes. They are spraying you with water.

<It is a *B'heeon*!> Ax cries. <Look out for it's —>

A three-foot-wide, sticky pink tongue suddenly shoots out of the creature's mouth. It laps you up like cream. You thrash about, but you can't escape as the tongue shoots you backward into the waiting mouth.

<Frog's legs. Delicious,> Visser Three says. And SLURP — you're finished.

Oops. Try again. Turn back to page 100.

CHAPTER 27

The jaguar owns the rain forest. You realize this as you take control of the morph. You feel the power of your coiled muscles, ready to spring. Your gaze can pick out details in the darkest shadow. You spy the tiniest beetle and the sloth hanging above you and the parrot in the tree.

They don't concern you. When you are hungry, you kill to eat. It is the way of the forest. You have power and control and grace and mobility and will.

<I feel pretty supreme,> Marco says. <I mean, I'm a pretty supreme human. But as a jaguar, I'm incredible.>

114

<The forest is incredible,> Cassie says softly. <It's layered with life.>

You know what she means. From the dirt underneath your pads to the tiniest branches overhead, the rain forest teems with life.

<How can the Hork-Bajir just slash and burn this place?> Rachel asks. <It's so incredible.>

<That is why we must stop them,> Ax says. <Wait.>

You pause. Your ears have picked up the same sounds.

<To the right,> Jake says.

<No,> Ax says. <We are surrounded.>

The Hork-Bajir have fanned out in the forest. They have made a pincer movement, and you have fallen into the trap.

Dracon beams explode around you. One of the Hork-Bajir swipes at Cassie, and she snarls and jumps at them. Rachel isn't far behind.

You spring at the neck of a Hork-Bajir, and it goes down. You swipe at another with your claws, and it howls and falls back. You fight with claws and teeth and all the power of the jaguar, but there are more of them than you.

<Fall back!> Jake cries. <The tribe must be behind us somewhere. They'll help!>

You leap onto a tree in order to hurl yourself on a Hork-Bajir. You climb up the vines, your paws digging in. But then the vines move. They surround you.

It is Visser Three in *Lerdethak* morph. He squeezes you. You feel your lungs collapsing. You feel something deep within you burst.

<Jake,> you call weakly.

Jake turns. You look into yellow jaguar eyes that suddenly seem human to you. They are full of sorrow.

And you know it's too late.